The Poet and the Composer

By

E. T. A. Hoffmann

British Library Cataloguing-in-Publication Data
A catalogue record for this book is available from the
British Library

E. T. A. Hoffman

Ernst Theodor Wilhelm Hoffmann was born in Königsberg, East Prussia in 1776. His family were all jurists, and during his youth he was initially encouraged to pursue a career in law. However, in his late teens Hoffman became increasingly interested in literature and philosophy, and spent much of his time reading German classicists and attending lectures by, amongst others, Immanuel Kant.

In was in his twenties, upon moving with his uncle to Berlin, that Hoffman first began to promote himself as a composer, writing an operetta called Die Maske and entering a number of playwriting competitions. Hoffman struggled to establish himself anywhere for a while, flitting between a number of cities and dodging the attentions of Napoleon's occupying troops. In 1808, while living in Bamberg, he began his job as a theatre manager and a music critic, and Hoffman's break came a year later, with the publication of Ritter Gluck. The story centred on a man who meets, or thinks he has met, a long-dead composer, and played into the 'doppelgänger' theme – at that time very popular in literature. It was shortly after this that Hoffman began to use the pseudonym E. T. A. Hoffmann, declaring the 'A' to stand for 'Amadeus', as a tribute to the great composer, Mozart.

Over the next decade, while moving between Dresden, Leipzig and Berlin, Hoffman produced a great range of both literary and musical works. Probably Hoffman's most well-known story, produced in 1816, is 'The Nutcracker and the Mouse King', due to the fact that – some seventy-six years later - it inspired Tchaikovsky's ballet The Nutcracker.

In the same vein, his story 'The Sandman' provided both the inspiration for Léo Delibes's ballet Coppélia, and the basis for a highly influential essay by Sigmund Freud, called 'The Uncanny'. (Indeed, Freud referred to Hoffman as the "unrivalled master of the uncanny in literature.")

Alcohol abuse and syphilis eventually took a great toll on Hoffman though, and – having spent the last year of his life paralysed – he died in Berlin in 1822, aged just 46. His legacy is a powerful one, however: He is seen as a pioneer of both Romanticism and fantasy literature, and his novella, Mademoiselle de Scudéri: A Tale from the Times of Louis XIV is often cited as the first ever detective story.

The Poet and the Composer

"**The** enemy was before the gates. Heavy guns were thundering in every direction, and shells were hurtling through the air; the people of the town were running, with white faces, into their houses, and the empty streets rang to the tramp of the cavalry patrols that were cantering along through them, and driving, with threats and curses, such of the soldiers as were loitering, or had fallen out of the ranks from any cause, forward into the trenches. But Ludwig sat on, in his back room, sunk and lost in the lovely, glorious vision-world which had opened upon him at his piano. For he had just completed a symphony, in which he had tried to write down, in notes to be seen and read, what he had heard and seen within him; a work which, like Beethoven's colossal ones in that kind, should tell, in heavenly language, of the glorious wonders of that far-off, romantic realm where life is all unspeakable, blissful, longing. Like his marvellous creations, it was to come from that far-off realm, into this little, arid, thirsty world of ours, and, with beautiful, syren-accents, lure away from it those who should list, and give ear to its charming. But the landlady came in and rated him for sitting at his piano in that time of danger and distress; asking him if he meant to stay in his garret and be shot. At first he didn't understand what the woman was talking about, till a fragment of a shell knocked a piece of the roof off, and the broken panes of the window went clattering down upon the floor. Then the landlady ran down-stairs weeping and screaming; and Ludwig, taking his most precious possession, the score of his symphony, under his arm, hastened after her to the cellar. The inhabitants of the house were all assembled there. In an access of liberality very unusual with him, the wine-shop keeper, who occupied the lower story, had 'stood' a dozen or so of his best wine; whilst the women, in fear and trembling, brought numerous tit-bits in their work-baskets. People ate and drank, and quickly passed from their condition of exaltation and excitement to that confidential frame of mind in which neighbour, drawing close to neighbour, seeks, and thinks he finds security; and, so to say, all the petty, artificial pas which we have been taught by conventionality are whelmed and merged in the great colossal waltz-whirl, to which the iron hand of destiny beats the resistless measure. The trouble and danger--the risk to life and limb--were forgotten; cheerful conversation was the order of the day; animated lips uttered brilliant speeches, and fellow-lodgers, who barely touched a hat to each other at ordinary times as they met on the stairs, were seated side by side, confiding to each other their most confidential affairs.

"The firing began to slacken a good deal, and there was talk of going up-stairs again, as the streets seemed to be getting pretty safe. An ex-Militaire, who was present, went further; and, after a few instructive observations concerning the system of fortification practised by the Romans, and the effect of the catapult (with a passing allusion or two to Vauban, and more modern times), was just proving to us that we had no cause for the slightest uneasiness, because the house was completely out of the line of fire, when a shot sent the bricks of the cellar-ventilator rattling down about our ears. No one was hurt, however; and, as the Militaire jumped, with a brimming bumper in his hand, on to the table (which the falling bricks had cleared of the bottles), and defied any other shot to trouble us, we were all quite reassured at once; and this proved to be our last scare. The night passed away quietly, and, in the morning, we found that the troops had moved off to occupy another position, abandoning the town to the enemy. On leaving the cellar, we found the enemy's cavalry scouring the streets, and a placard posted up guaranteeing that the townsfolk and their property should not be molested.

"Ludwig joined the throng, eager to see the new spectacle, which was watching the arrival of the enemy's commander-in-chief, who was coming in at the gate, with a pompous fanfare of trumpets, surrounded by a brilliant escort. Scarcely could he believe his eyes when he saw his old college-friend Ferdinand among the staff, in a quiet-looking uniform, with his left arm in a sling, curvetting close past him on a beautiful sorrel charger. 'It was he--it was really and truly himself and no other!' Ludwig cried involuntarily. He couldn't overtake him, his horse was going too fast, and Ludwig hastened, full of thought, back to his room. But he couldn't get on with any work; he could think of nothing but his old friend, whom he had not seen for years; and the happy days of youth which they had spent together rose to his memory bright and clear. At that time Ferdinand had never shown any turn for soldiering: he was devoted to the Muses, and had evinced his poetic vocation in many a striking poem; so that this transformation was all the more incomprehensible; and Ludwig burned with anxiety to speak with him, though he had no notion where or how he should find him. The bustle and movement in the streets increased; a considerable portion of the enemy's forces, with the Allied Princes at their head, passed through the town, as a halt was to be made in the neighbourhood for a day or two; and the greater the crowd about headquarters the less chance there seemed of encountering Ferdinand. But suddenly, in an out-of-the-way café, where Ludwig was in the habit of going for his frugal dinner, Ferdinand came up to him with a cry of delight.

"Ludwig was silent, for a certain feeling of discomfort embittered, for him, this longed-for meeting. It was, as it often is in dreams, when, just as we are going to put our arms about people whom we love, they suddenly change into something else, and the whole thing becomes a mockery, Here was the gentle son of the Muses, the writer of many a romantic lay which Ludwig had clothed in music, in a nodding plume, with a clanking sword at his side, and even his voice transformed to a harsh, rough tone of command. Ludwig's gloomy glance rested on the wounded arm, and upon the decoration, the cross of honour, on his breast. But Ferdinand put his arm round him and pressed him to his side.

"'I know what you are thinking,' he said; 'I understand

10

what you feel at this meeting of ours. But the Fatherland called me; I could not hesitate to obey. My hand, which had only wielded the pen, took up the sword, with the joy, with the enthusiasm, which the holy cause has kindled in every breast which is not stamped with the seal of cowardice. I have given some of my blood already; and the mere accident that this happened under the Prince's eyes has gained me this cross. But, believe me, Ludwig, the strings which vibrated in me of old, and whose tones have so often spoken to you, are all whole and uninjured still; and many a night, when, after some fierce engagement, the troopers have been sleeping round the fire of the bivouac on some lonely picquet, I have written poems which have elevated me and inspired me in my glorious duty of fighting for Honour and Freedom.'

"Ludwig's heart opened at these words; and when Ferdinand went with him into a small private room, and took off his sword and helmet, he felt as if his friend had only been dressed to act a part, and had taken off his stage-costume.

"As they dined and talked over the old days they began to feel as if they had only parted yesterday. Ferdinand asked what Ludwig had been composing lately, and was much astonished to learn that he had never written an opera, because he never had been able to meet with a libretto to his satisfaction--one that could inspire him with music.

"'I can't understand,' said Ferdinand, 'why you haven't written a Libretto long ago yourself. You have a very vivid imagination, and a fine command of language.'

"Ludwig. 'Yes, I have imagination enough to invent plenty of good plots. Indeed, often, when at night a slight headache keeps me in that dreamy condition which is like a struggle between sleeping and waking, I not only think of splendid subjects for operas, but see and hear them being performed, to my own music. But, so far as the faculty of retaining them and writing them down is concerned, my belief is that I am wholly without it. And in fact it is scarcely to be expected of us composers that we should acquire that technical, mechanical skill (which is necessary to success in every art, and only comes by constant perseverance and long practice) which would enable us to write our own librettos. But even if I had the skill to write out a plot, properly arranged in lines, scenes, etc., I scarcely think I should set to work to do it for myself.'

"Ferdinand. 'But then nobody could so thoroughly understand your special musical tendencies as yourself.'

"Ludwig. 'That, I daresay, may be true enough. Still, I can't help thinking that a composer who should sit down to put the idea of a plot, which had occurred to him, into the words would be something like a painter who should be called upon to make a minute etching, or a line-engraving, of his picture before setting to work to draw it and colour it.'

"Ferdinand. 'You mean that the necessary fire would smoulder out during the process of versifying?'

"Ludwig. 'I think it would. My poetry would seem trashy, to myself; something like the cases of rockets which had fallen down, charred and empty, after rushing all resplendent up to the skies. To me it appears that in no art so much as in music is it so essential that the entirety of the subject involved, with all its parts, down to the minutest detail, should be grasped by the mind at first, in its earliest, glowing outburst; because in no other is subsequent polishing and altering so hurtful. I am convinced, by my own experience, that the melody which comes to you, as at the wave of an enchanter's wand, the first time you read the words of a poem, is always the best--nay, probably the only really right one (for that particular composer at all events), to put to it. It would be impossible for a composer not to think of the music called for by the situation, while he was writing down the words. Indeed he would be thinking so much of it that he could not give the necessary attention to the words, and if he forced himself to do so the river of the music would soon dry up, as if sucked in by thirsty sands. Nay, to express my meaning more clearly, I will say that, at the moment of his musical inspiration, all words, all verbal expressions, would appear insufficient to him, nay flat, and miserably inadequate; and it would be necessary for him to come down to a lower level, to go, like a beggar asking for alms, in quest of those words, necessities of the lower requirements of his existence. Would not his wings soon be paralysed, like a caged eagle's, so that he would try to soar sunwards in vain?'

"Ferdinand. 'One listens to all this, of course; but do you know, my dear friend, that what you say does not so much convince me as it seems to indicate your own personal repugnance to working your way, laboriously, through all the necessary scenas, arias, duettos, etc., till you get to the point of composing the music.'

"Ludwig. 'Perhaps; but I renew an old reproach. Why, in the days when you and I were living in such constant intimacy, would you never write me a libretto, eagerly as I begged you to do so?'

"Ferdinand. 'Because I think it the most thankless labour imaginable. You must allow that no demands could be more exacting than those which you composers make upon us; and if you say that a musician can't be expected to acquire the technical skill which the mechanical part of poetry-writing demands, I, again, think that it is too much to expect of a poet that he should be continually harassing himself about the precise structure of your terzettes, quartettes, finales, etc., so as not to run the risk of transgressing against some of those forms, which you look upon--Heaven knows why--as so many matters fixed and established for ever and ever, like the laws of the Medes and Persians. After we have expended our best efforts with extremity of mental tension, in trying to apprehend all the situations of our story in a true poetical spirit, and to express them in the most eloquent language, and the smoothest and most finished versification, it is quite terrible how you run your pens through our finest lines, in the most relentless manner, and spoil our happiest ideas and expressions, by inverting them, or altering them, or drowning them in the music. I say this merely with reference to the uselessness of spending time and labour on elaborate finish. But then, many admirable plots, which have occurred to us in our poetic inspiration, and which we bring to you, all pride, expecting you to be delighted with them, you reject in a moment, as being unsuitable, and unworthy to be clothed in music. But this must often be sheer caprice, or I don't know what else it can be; because you often set to work upon texts which are absolutely wretched and----'

"Ludwig. 'Stop a moment, my dear friend! Of course there are composers who have as little idea of music as many rhyme-spinners have of poetry, and they have often put notes to plots which really are wretched, in all respects. But real composers, who live and move and have their being in true, glorious, heavenly Music, always choose poetic texts.'

"Ferdinand. 'Do you say so of Mozart?'

"Ludwig. 'Mozart--however paradoxical it may appear to you--never chose any but poetic texts for his classical operas. But, leaving that on one side for the moment, my opinion is that it is always quite easy to know what sort of plot is adapted for an opera, so that the poet need never be in any danger of making any mistake about it.'

"Ferdinand. 'I must confess I never have really gone into this: and indeed I know so little about music that I don't suppose it would have been of much consequence if I had.'

"Ludwig. 'If by the expression "knowing about music" you mean being thoroughly versed in the so-called "school routine" of music, there is no necessity for your being that, to be able to know what composers require. It is quite easy, altogether apart from the school routine, so to comprehend, and have within one, the true essence of music as to be, in

15

this sense, a much better musician than a person who, after studying the whole, extensive school-routine in the sweat of his forehead, and labouring through all its manifold, intricate mazes and labyrinths, worships its lifeless rules and regulations as a self-manufactured Fetish, in place of the living Spirit: and whom this Idol-cult excludes from the happiness of the higher realm of bliss.'

"Ferdinand. 'Then you think the poet might enter into this inner sanctum without the preliminary initiation of the "school"?'

"Ludwig. 'I do, certainly. And I say that, in that far-off realm which we often feel,--so dimly, but so unmistakeably,--to be so close about us, whence marvellous voices sound to us, awakening all the tones which are sleeping in our hearts, cabined, cribbed, confined, so that those tones, awakened and set free, dart aloft in fiery streams, gladsome and happy, and we taste of the bliss of that paradise whence the voices come--I say that, in that far-off realm, the Poet and the Musician are intimately-allied members of one and the same Church: for the "secret" of poetry and of music is one and the same, and opens to both the portals of the Inner Sanctuary.'

"Ferdinand. 'I hear my dear old Ludwig trying to formulate the laws of art in dim and mystic phrases; and I must say, that the gulf which seemed to lie between poet and composer, begins to look much narrower than it did.'

"Ludwig. 'Let me try to express my idea about the true essentials of Opera in as few words as possible. A proper opera, in my opinion, is one in which the music springs directly out of the poem, as a necessary sequence, or consequence.'

"Ferdinand. 'I don't quite understand that, as yet.'

"Ludwig. 'Is not music the mysterious language of a higher spirit-realm, whose wondrous accents make their way into our souls, awaking in them a higher Intensivity of life? All passions contend together, shimmering in bright armour, and then merge and sink into an ineffable longing which fills our being. This is the effect (not, perhaps, to be more clearly expressed in words) of Instrumental music. But Music, to enter wholly into our lives, must take those visions of hers which she thus brings with her, and, clothing them in words and actions, speak to us of particular passions and events. Very well! Can the vulgar and the common-place be spoken of in those accents of glory? Can Music tell us of anything other than the wonders and the mysteries of that realm from whence she comes to us with those magic tones of hers? Let the poet equip himself for a bold flight into the land of romance. There he will find the Marvellous, which it is for him to bring into this work-a-day world, so living and glowing in brilliant colouring that we accept it as true without hesitation. So that--as if carried out of this arid every-day life in some blissful dream--we go wandering along the flowery paths of that happy country, and, forgetting everything else for the time, understand its language--which is what the mighty voice of Music speaks.'

"Ferdinand. 'Then it is the Romantic Opera, with its fairies and spirits, its prodigies and transformations, that you would adhere to, exclusively?'

"Ludwig. 'I certainly think the Romantic Opera the only perfect kind, because it is only in the realm of the Romantic that music is at home. Of course you will understand that I profoundly despise that miserable class of productions in which silly, unspiritual spirits appear, and where wonders are heaped upon wonders, without rhyme or reason, merely for the delectation of the eyes of the musical groundlings. It is only a poet of true genius who can write the book of a proper Romantic Opera; for none other can bring the wonders of the Spirits-World into this life of ours. On his wings we soar across the gulf which divides us from it. We grow to feel at home in that strange land; we give belief to the marvels which, as necessary results of the influence of higher natures on our personality, we see taking place; and we comprehend all the powerful incidents and situations which fill us with awe and horror, and also with the highest rapture. It is, in one word, the magical power of Poetical Truth which the poet who would represent those marvels must have at his command; for it is that alone which can carry us away: and a mere collection of meaningless fairies, who (as is the case in so many productions of the kind) are introduced only to dance about the pagliasso in flesh-coloured skin-tights,--foolish absurdities as they are,--will always leave us indifferent and uninterested. In an opera the effect produced upon us by the influence of higher beings should take place visibly, so as to display before our eyes a romantic life, or condition of existence, in which the language, too, is more highly potentiated; or rather, is derived from that distant realm: in other words, is sung music: ay! where the scenes and incidents, too, hovering and soaring about in grand and beautiful tones, and masses of tones, seize us and carry us away with irresistible might. It is in this way that, as I said before, the music ought to take its rise and origin straight out of the poem, as a necessary sequence, or consequence.'

"Ferdinand. 'Now I quite understand you; and I think, at once, of Tasso and Ariosto. Still, it seems to me, it would be no easy matter to write a musical drama as you would postulate it.'

"Ludwig. 'It is work for a real romantic poet, of true genius. Think of the splendid Gozzi! in his dramatic legends he has completely fulfilled the conditions which I have laid down as essential for the poet of opera, and I cannot understand why this rich mine of magnificent opera-plots has been so little drawn upon, hitherto.'

"Ferdinand. 'I remember being greatly delighted with Gozzi, when I read him some years ago; though, of course, I did not then look at him from your point of view.'

"Ludwig. 'One of the best of his tales is "The Raven." A certain King Millo, of Frattombrosa, cares for nothing but the chase. One day in the forest he sees a splendid raven, and he sends an arrow through its heart. The raven falls upon a monumental tomb of the whitest marble, which there is there under the trees, besprinkling it with his blood. On this, the forest is shaken, as if by an earthquake; and a terrible monster comes stalking out of a cave, and thunders forth a curse upon Millo, in the following terms:--

19

"Findest thou not a fair woman,
White as this monument's marble,
Red as the raven's heart's blood,
Black as the night of his plumes,
Perish in raving madness."

"'All attempts to discover such a woman are fruitless. But the king's brother, Gennaro, who is devoted to him, vows that he will never rest till he finds this woman, who is to restore his brother's reason. He traverses land and sea; till at last, counselled by an old man versed in necromancy, he discovers Armilla, daughter of the mighty sorcerer Norand. White is her skin like the monument's marble, red like the raven's blood; and black as his plumes are her hair and eyebrows. He succeeds in carrying her off, and after many adventures, they reach the shores of Frattombrosa in safety. As he lands on the beach, chance places in his possession a magnificent charger, and a falcon endowed with extraordinary powers. He is filled with joy that he is enabled to restore his brother's reason, and also to have two such acceptable gifts to offer him. He lies down to rest in a pavilion which has been prepared for him under a tree. Then two doves come and sit in the branches, and begin to talk:--

"'"Woe! Woe to Gennaro! Well had he never been born; the falcon will peck out his brother's eyes--but if he giveth it not, or if he telleth what he hath heard, he will turn to stone; if his brother mounteth the horse, it will instantly kill him-- but if he giveth it not, or telleth what he hath heard, he will turn to stone; if his brother weddeth Armilla, a monster will come on the wedding-night, and tear him limb from limb but if Gennaro withholdeth Armilla, or telleth what he hath heard, he will turn to stone!

""'Woe! Woe to Gennaro! Well had he never been born!"

"'Norand appears, and confirms what the doves have said. It is the punishment--the penalty, for having carried Armilla away.

"'As soon as Millo sets eyes on Armilla, his madness departs. The horse and the hawk are brought, and the king is charmed with his brother's affection in bringing him presents so much to his mind. Gennaro brings the hawk, but ere his brother can take it, he cuts off its head. Thus Millo's eyes are saved; and just as Millo is setting foot in the stirrup to mount the horse, Gennaro draws his sword and hews off its fore-legs with one stroke. Millo thinks it is love-madness which causes Gennaro's conduct, and Armilla confirms this opinion, as Gennaro's sighs and tears, and his confusion and inexplicable behaviour have for some time made her suspect him of being secretly in love with her. She assures the king of her entire devotion to him; of which Gennaro had laid the foundation, by his warm and touching accounts of his brother on the journey. To cast aside all suspicion, she begs that the marriage may be hurried on as much as possible; and that is accordingly done. Gennaro, who sees his brother's last hours at hand, is in despair at being so misjudged; and yet, a terrible fate awaits him if a word of explanation crosses his lips. But he determines to save his brother, at whatever cost, and makes his way in the night, by a subterranean passage, to his sleeping chamber. A terrible dragon appears, breathing flames and fire. Gennaro attacks it; but his blows have no effect; the monster is nearing the sleeping chamber. In his desperation he delivers a tremendous two-handed stroke at the creature, and this cleaves through the door of the chamber. Millo comes out, and, as the monster has disappeared, he sees in his brother a traitor urged to fratricide by the madness of unhallowed passion. Gennaro cannot vindicate himself. The guards are summoned, and he is disarmed and thrown into a dungeon. He is doomed to die, but begs that he may speak with his brother first. Millo consents. Gennaro recalls to his memory the tender affection which has always subsisted between them; but when he asks if his brother can truly suppose him capable of his murder, Millo calls for proofs of his innocence; and then, in his agony, Gennaro divulges the terrible prophecies of the doves and Norand. But no sooner have the words been spoken than Gennaro is turned to a marble statue. On this Millo, in his grief and remorse, determines that he never will leave the statue's side, and will die at its feet in contrition and sorrow. At this juncture Norand appears, and says, "In the eternal Book of Destiny were written the raven's death, the curse on you, and the carrying away of Armilla. One thing, and one alone, will bring your brother back to life--but it is a terrible deed. Let Armilla be slain at the statue's side, by this dagger; and when the cold marble is besprinkled with her heart's blood, it will warm into life. If you have courage to kill her, do it. Weep, weep, and lament! even as do I!" He vanishes. Armilla wrings from the unfortunate Millo the purport of Norand's terrible disclosure. Millo quits her in despair, and, filled with horror and grief, careless of living longer, she stabs herself with the dagger. As soon as her blood besprinkles the statue Gennaro comes back to life. Millo comes: he sees his brother alive, and his bride lying slain. In his despair he is going to stab himself with the dagger; but the gloomy dungeon changes to a great, illuminated hall; Norand appears: all the mysterious decrees of fate are accomplished, all the sorrow is past. Norand touches Armilla. She comes back to life, and everything ends happily.'

"Ferdinand. 'Yes; I remember this fine, imaginative tale quite well, and the impression it made upon me. You are quite right; this is an instance in which the Marvellous takes the form of an essential element, and has so much poetical verity that we believe it without hesitation. Millo's killing of the raven is what knocks at the brazen gates of the Spirit-Realm; on that they fly open with a clash, and the spirits come swooping in upon the human life, and immesh the mortals in the web of strange, mysterious destiny which impends over them.'

"Ludwig. 'Exactly; and notice the grand, powerful situations which the poet has evolved from this contest with the spirit-world. Gennaro's self-sacrifice; Armilla's deed of heroism; there is a grandeur in them which our "moral" playwrights, in their rummagings among the paltrinesses of every-day life (like sweepings of drawing-rooms thrown out into the dust-bin) haven't the slightest idea of; and then the comic parts for the masks are must effectively woven in.'

"Ferdinand. 'Yes it is only in the Romantic Drama that the comic element blends on such perfectly equal terms with the tragic that they contribute with equality to the general effect.'

"Ludwig. Even common opera-manufacturers have got hold of some dim notion of that, for it is thence that the so-called Comic-Heroic operas take their origin--productions in which the Heroic is often exceedingly Comic, and the Comic is so far Heroic that it most heroically ignores all the requirements of taste and propriety.'

"Ferdinand. 'According to your notion of the essentials of opera, we can't congratulate ourselves on possessing very many.'

"Ludwig. 'No; most so-called operas are only plays with singing added; and the utter absence of dramatic effect, which is ascribed sometimes to the music, sometimes to the plot or to the words, is really due to the lifelessness of the mass of scenes, tacked together without inward connection or poetical truthfulness, and incapable of kindling music into life. The composer has often to work between the lines, as it were, on his own account, and the wretched words meander along in a side-channel, not to be brought into the musical current by any conceivable means. In such a case the music may be good enough; that is,--without having depth enough to carry away the listener with magic power, it may give a certain amount of pleasure, like a glittering play of gay colours. Then the opera is merely a concert, given on a stage, with dresses and scenery.'

"Ferdinand. 'As it is the Romantic Opera, in its strictest sense, which is the only species that you recognise as opera, properly so-called, how about musical Tragedies, and Comic Operas in modern costume?--you repudiate them altogether, I presume.'

"Ludwig. 'Oh, no; not at all. In most of the older Tragic Operas--such as are not written nowadays, unfortunately (either as regards plots or music)--what so powerfully sways the audience is the heroic nature of the action, and the inward strength of the characters and situations. That dark mysterious power which rules, controls, and disposes of Gods and Men, we see stalking along visibly before our eyes; we hear the eternal, irreversible, immutable decrees of Fate, to which the Gods themselves have to submit, pronounced and formulated aloud, in awful and mysterious tones. From Tragic matter of this sort the Fantastic element is perforce excluded; but a loftier language--in the wondrous accents of Music--has to be employed to depict that intercourse with the Gods which stirs the Mortals to a higher life, and to God-like achievements. Were not the ancient tragedies musically declaimed, by the way?--and did not that prove clearly the necessity for a higher medium of expression than ordinary language? The musical tragedies have inspired composers of genius in a quite special way--with a lofty, I might almost say, a saintly style of writing. It is as if we mortals were wafted upwards, in some condition of mystic consecration, on the pinions of the tones of the golden harps of the Cherubim and Seraphim, to the realms of light, where we learn the mystery of our existence. What I would say, Ferdinand, is to point out the close relationship that there is between the old Church Style and the Tragic Opera, whence the old writers have framed a glorious style of their own, of which modern composers have no idea--not even excepting Spontini, with all his wealth and exuberance of fancy. The glorious Gluck, who stands apart by himself, a hero, I need say nothing about; but as an instance how the grand tragic style has influenced far inferior talents, think of the chorus of the Priests of Night in Piccini's "Dido.'"

"Ferdinand. 'This is just as it used to be in the golden old days when we were together. As you talk in that inspired sort of way of your Art, you raise me up to the level of ideas which otherwise I never should have dreamt of; and, I assure you, at this moment I consider that I really know a good deal about music. In fact, I think no passable line of poetry would occur to me without its appropriate clothing of music.'

"Ludwig. 'Is not this the true inspiration of the poet of opera? I maintain that he should "think" the music belonging to his lines just as much>as the composer does; and that the only thing which differentiates the one from the other is the distinct recognition of particular melodies, and of particular qualities and peculiarities of the Bounds of instruments which are co-operating and involved in the effects; in fact, the easy, habitual command over the "Inner Kingdom" of Music. But I have still to tell you my ideas about Opera Buffa.'

"Ferdinand. 'You will scarcely have a good word to say for

that, particularly if it is in modern costume.'

"Ludwig. 'On the contrary, I consider that it is just when it is in the costume of the day that not only is it at its best, but that it is the only genuine form of opera buffa in the sense in which the mobile, mercurial, excitable Italians have understood it and written it. In this case it is the Fantastic element which is paramount, proceeding partly from the quips of individual characters, partly from the bizarre play of chance. The Fantastic element comes pop into our everyday lives, and turns everything topsy-turvy. One ought to have to say, "Yes; that really is Brown (or Jones, or Robinson) in that snuff-coloured Sunday coat of his with the brass buttons, which we all know so well. And what in the name of fortune 's the fellow going on like that for?" Picture to yourself some respectable family--uncles, aunts, and so forth--and a little languishing daughter; throw in two or three students, be-singing their cousin's eyes and playing the guitar under the windows. Let the tricksy sprite Puck pop suddenly into the middle of them! The result you may imagine. All the fat's in the fire; everything is at sixes and sevens; everybody goes darting in every direction, gesticulating and grimacing, skipping and posturing, as if a whole hive of bees were let loose in their bonnets. Some strange planet rules the ascendant; the nets of haphazard are set, and will catch the most respectable folk if their noses happen to be just the least bit longer than the average. I consider that the very essence of opera buffa lies in this incursion of the Fanciful-Fantastic, the preposterous and absurd, into actual, everyday life, and the incongruities that result. And it is just the power of catching hold of this fanciful-fantastic element--which generally lies rather far off and out of the way--and bringing it, with vividness, into everyday life, which makes the acting of Italian buffo actors so inimitable. They catch the indications given by the author, and their acting clothes the skeleton which he has sketched with flesh and colour.'

"Ferdinand. 'I think I follow you quite. What you mean is, that in the opera buffa the Fantastic element takes the place of the Romantic (which, in general terms, you consider an essential principle of opera), and the art of the poet has to consist in this--that the characters must appear, not only with much finish, and standing out in alto-relievo, as well as being poetically true, but so clearly drawn as well from everyday life, and so full of individual character, that the spectator at once says, "Look there! that's my next-door neighbour, whom I say 'How are you?' to every day. And that's the student who goes to his lectures every morning, and sighs so tremendously as he passes his cousin's window," etc., etc. And then all these people are to be subjected to the spell of some Puck, in such fashion that what they set to work to do under that influence, and all that happens to them, are to affect us as if we were there on the spot, sharing their experiences with them, under the influence of the same spell.'

"Ludwig. 'Exactly. And I scarcely need say that, according to my principle, music adapts itself well to opera buffa, and that in so adapting itself there results a certain special style which makes a special impression of its own on the hearer.'

"Ferdinand. 'Do you think music can express all the shades of the Comic?'

"Ludwig. 'I am quite sure it can; clever artists have proved it scores of times. For instance, music can express the most delicate and delightful Irony. That is the predominating element in Mozart's glorious "Cosi fan tutte."'

"Ferdinand. That, by the way, leads me to the remark that, according to your principle, the so-much disparaged text of that work is really highly suitable for an opera.'

"Ludwig. 'That is exactly what I was thinking of when I said, a little while ago, that for his classic operas Mozart always chose really suitable texts, for "Le Nozze di Figaro" is more a Comedy in Music than a true Opera. The nefarious attempt to turn pathetic dramas into operas can never come to anything; our "Orphan Hospitals," "Oculists," and so forth, are sure to be soon forgotten. And what could have been more miserable and opposed to the true spirit of opera than all that series of vaudeilles of Dittersdorf's? But on the other hand I call such works as "The Sunday-Child" and "The Sisters of Prague" admirable. One might style them true German opere buffe.'

"Ferdinand. 'They have always amused me greatly, at all events, when decently given; and I have always thought of what Tieck makes his "poet" say to the public in his "Puss in Boots": "If you want to enjoy this thoroughly, you must divest yourself of whatever you may have attained in the shape of cultivation and learning, and become wholly as little children, so as to enjoy it as such."'

"Ludwig. 'Unfortunately those words, like many others of the kind, fell upon stony ground, and could take no root. But the vox populi, which is generally the vox Dei in theatrical matters, has drowned the few isolated sighs and groans which super-delicate and sensitive people have given vent to over the sad untruthfulness and tastelessness of those works--"trifling," according to their ideas. And there are instances on record of some of those very people who, in the height of their calm, contemptuous, aristocratic impassibility and supercilious scorn of the whole thing, have been so carried away by the infection of the roars of laughter of the "baser" folk about them that they have burst out laughing in the most deplorable way themselves, declaring that they had no idea what they were laughing at.'

"Ferdinand. 'Wouldn't Tieck, if he had chosen, have written splendid opera plots, according to your definition of them?'

"Ludwig. 'No doubt, being a true romantic poet; and I remember I did once think of writing music to a plot of his. But though the subject was well adapted for music, the work was too diffuse and lengthy; not concentrated enough. It was called "The Monster of the Enchanted Forest," if I remember rightly.'

"Ferdinand. 'That reminds me of another difficulty which we meet with in writing for you composers: I mean the extraordinary brevity and conciseness which you insist upon. All our efforts to portray this or that situation or burst of passion in properly descriptive language are so much wasted

30

labour. You will have the whole affair comprised in a line or two; and even these few lines you twist about and turn upside-down just as you take it in your heads.'

"Ludwig. 'I think the writer of the words of an opera ought to be something like a scene painter, and paint his picture correctly as regards the drawing, but in broad, powerful lines; then the music will be what will make it appear in proper light and shade, and in correct perspective, so that it shall have a proper effect of life, and what seemed only meaningless dashes of colour prove to be forms instinct with meaning, standing out prominently in relief.'

"Ferdinand. 'So that what we have to do is to give you a sketch merely, not a finished poem?'

"Ludwig. 'No, no; that is not what I mean at all! It is scarcely necessary to say that the poet of opera must observe, as regards the arrangement, the disposition, of the whole, all the rules essential to dramatic composition; but what he has to take special care for is to so order his scenes that the subject-matter may unfold itself, clearly and intelligibly, to the eyes of the spectator: who ought to be able to understand what is going on from what he sees taking place, almost without catching any of the words. No dramatic poem so absolutely demands this sort of distinctness as the opera-text, for not only is it more difficult to distinguish words when they are sung, (however distinctly,) than when they are spoken, but the music tends to carry the audience into distant regions, and it is necessary that the attention should be kept directed to the particular point whore the action is concentrated, pro tempore. Then as regards the words, the composer likes them best when they express the passion, or situation, to which they refer, vigorously and concisely. There is no occasion for flowery diction, and, above all, there should be no imagery, no similes.'

"Ferdinand. 'Then how about Metastasio, with his exuberance of similes?'

"Ludwig. 'Yes; he had the strange idea that the composer, particularly in arias, must always have his imagination stirred up by some poetical comparison. Hence his oft-repeated openings such as "Come una Tortorella," etc., or "Come Spume in Tempesta," etc.: and in fact, the cooing of doves and the roar of the sea have often made their appearance--in the accompaniment, at all events.'

"Ferdinand. 'But, while we avoid flowery language, are we to be allowed any sort of elaboration of interesting situations? For instance: the young hero sets off to the battle, and bids adieu to his aged father, the old king, whose country is trembling in the grasp of a victorious usurper. Or some terrible fate severs a youth from his beloved. Are neither of them to say anything but just "fare-thee-well"?'

"Ludwig. 'The hero may add a few words about his courage and the justice of his cause, and the lover may tell his sweetheart that life will be nothing but a long, painful dream without her. Still, the simple "fare-thee-well" will be amply sufficient for the Composer--(who draws his inspiration, not from the words, but from the business and the situations)-- to represent the mental condition of the hero and the lover with powerful strokes and touches. To stick to the instance you have adduced; just think in what thousands of most affecting and heart-breaking ways the Italians have sung the little word "addio." What thousands--ay, and thousands of thousands--of shades musical expression is capable of! And of course it is just that that is the marvellous mystery of the Tone-Art that, just where language comes to an end, she is only beginning to disclose a perennial fountain of fresh forms of expression.'

"Ferdinand. 'Then what the opera-poet has to do is--to strive to attain the utmost simplicity, as far as the words are concerned; it will be enough to suggest the situation, in clear and forcible language.'

"Ludwig. 'Exactly: because the composer has to draw his inspiration from the matter, the business and the situation--not from the words. And not only is imagery to be avoided, but everything in the shape of a reflection is a bugbear to the composer.'

"Ferdinand. 'After what you have said, I can assure you it seems to be anything but an easy matter to write an opera text. Now, this indispensable simpleness of the language; I can't say that I quite see how to----'

"Ludwig. 'How to accomplish it! No! You are so fond of painting with words, and so accustomed to it. But though Metastasio (as I think) has exemplified in his librettos how opera texts ought not to be written, there are quantities of Italian poems which are absolute models of words for music. For instance take the lines, known to the whole world, no doubt:

"Almen si non poss' io
Seguir l'amato bene,
Affetti del cor mio
Seguite-lo per me!"

What can be simpler? Yet, in these few, unpretending words lies the suggestion, or indication, of love and sorrow which the composer comprehends, and can apply all the resources of musical expression to represent. The particular situation in which the words are to be sung will so stir his imagination that he will give the music the most individual character. And this is why you will often find that a poetical composer sets words that are wretched enough to admirable music. In such cases what inspired him was that the matter was genuinely suitable for opera; and as an instance I merely mention Mozart's "Zauberfloete."'

"Ferdinand was going to reply, when, outside the windows, down in the street, the drums were heard beating the générale. This seemed to wake him to the sense of present duty as with an electric shock. Ludwig shook him warmly by the hand.

"'Ah, Ferdinand,' he cried, 'what is to become of Art in these terrible times? Won't it die, like some delicate plant lifting its languid head towards the clouds beyond which the sun has disappeared? Ah! Where are the golden days when we were lads? All that is good is drowned and swept away by this torrent that whirls along, devastating the country. We see bleeding corpses, appearing by glimpses, carried along in its dark billows; and in the horror which seizes us, we slip and lose our footing, we have nothing to hold on to; our cry of terror dies away in the darksome air--victims of inappeasable anger, we sink to earth, and there is no hope of salvation.' Ludwig paused, sunk in his thoughts.

"Ferdinand stood up, and put on his sword and helmet. He stood before Ludwig like the God of War armed for the fray. Ludwig looked up at him admiringly, and a glow came over Ferdinand's face, and he said, in a calm and reassuring tone:

"'Ludwig, what has happened to you? Has the dungeon air which you have been breathing here so long debilitated you, so that you are too sick and faint to feel the warm reviving breath of spring which is blowing, sweet and gentle, up there among the clouds as they glow with the rose tints of dawn? The children of Nature were abbrutized and sunk in sluggish inaction, careless of all her most precious gifts, and treading them into the mire. Then their angry mother awoke the Genius of War, who had long been sleeping in gardens heavy with the breath of flowers--and War came, like some Giant of Adamant, amongst these spoilt children, who, at the sound of his awful voice, which makes the hills tremble, fled to their mother's arms for refuge, though they had forgotten her before. But with remembrance came gratitude. Nothing but strength brings success. The divine element radiates out from contest and striving as life does from death. Yes, Ludwig, a time is upon us which is pregnant with fate, and (as in the awful profundity of the ancient Sagas, which come rolling over to us like the mysterious muttering of distant thunder) we can trace, once more, distinctly, the voice of that Power which rules for Ever more. Nay, marching visibly into our lives, it awakes in us a faith which enables us to read the riddle of our Being. The morning light is breaking, and inspired Singers are soaring up in the sweet fresh morning air, proclaiming the advent of the Divine, and celebrating it with hymns of praise. The golden gates are open, and art and knowledge, in one united ray, are kindling that flame of sacred effort which makes all humanity one universal Church. Therefore lift up your eyes, dear friend. Courage-- Confidence--Faith.'

"Ferdinand clasped Ludwig's hand; and in a few moments his charger was bearing him rapidly along with the troops moving on to the attack, the light and joy of battle on every brow."

The friends were much affected by this; for each of them remembered days when the clutch of a hostile destiny was at his throat and all comfort or enjoyment in life seemed to be a thing of the past for ever. And then, after a time, the first rays of the beautiful Star of Hope began to pierce the clouds and rose higher and higher, reviving them, strengthening and invigorating them with newness of life. Then, in the gladsomeness of contest, everything stirred, and came into activity, shouting for joy. At last the grandest and most brilliant of victories rewarded their courage and constancy.

"Each of us," said Lothair, "has said, within himself, very

much what the Serapiontic Ferdinand said; and well is it for us that the menacing storms which thundered over our heads refreshed us, instead of annihilating us, and braced us like a fine sulphur bath. In fact, it seems to me that it is only now, and here among you, that I begin to feel quite strong and well, and to trace a fresh impulse to begin, now that the storms are over, to bestir myself again in the paths of literature and science. I know that Theodore is doing so right strenuously; he is devoting himself, as of old, to his music, although he is not neglecting literature neither, so that I am expecting him to astonish us, one of these days, with an opera altogether his own, both music and words. All that he has said about the impossibility of the same person writing the words and the music of an opera may be plausible enough, but it doesn't convince me."

"I don't agree with you," said Cyprian, "but I don't see much use in continuing the discussion. It seems all the more a waste of time that if the thing were possible, which Theodore says it is not, he would be the first to set about doing it. It would be far better if he would open his piano and, as he has favoured us with so many interesting Stories, let us hear some of his Compositions."

"Cyprian," said Theodore, "is always accusing me of sticking too closely to established forms, and rejecting any poetry which cannot be fitted to some of them. This I do not admit, and I mean to prove what I say by producing some music of mine to words which require a setting differing from any of the hackneyed 'forms' in question. I mean the Night

37

Hymn in Mueller the painter's 'Genofeva.' All the sweet sadness,--the pain, longing, and sense of the supernatural,--of a heart torn by hopeless love are in the words of this beautiful poem. Moreover, as the verses have a certain touching flavour of the Antique, I have thought it better that the composition should be without any instrumental accompaniment, but for voices alone, in the style of old Alessandro Scarlatti, or the more modern Benedetto Marcello. I have done all the music for it in my head, but only the beginning of it has been written down as yet. If you haven't quite forgotten all about singing, and, especially, if you still feel the benefit of our old practice at 'reading invisible music,' and can strike your notes correctly as of old, I should like that we sing what I have composed for thebe words."

"Ah yes!" said Ottmar, "I remember about the 'reading invisible music.' You used to put your fingers on the notes of the chords without pressing them down, and each of us sang the notes of his part without previously hearing them on the instrument. People who didn't notice the process of indicating the notes couldn't imagine how we 'improvised' part-music so cleverly; and for those who possess the talent of being easily astonished, it really is a good and interesting musical trick. For my part, I still sing that mediocre, grumbling old baritone of mine, and have as little forgotten how to hit my note as Lothair, who can still, with his fine basso, lay firm foundations on which tenors like you and Cyprian can build skywards with security."

"For Cyprian's beautiful, delicate, tender tenor," said

Theodore, "this thing of mine is exactly suitable. Therefore I shall give him the first tenor part, and take the second myself. Ottmar, who was always very accurate in striking his note, shall take the first bass, and Lothair the second. Only, for Heaven's sake, don't thunder, but keep the whole thing soft and sostenuto, as the character of the composition requires."

Theodore struck two or three introductory chords on the piano, and then the voices began, with long, sustained notes, in the key of A flat major:

"Beauteous Lover's Star,
That gleamest far and far,
In pale blue vault of Heaven!
To thee, this night, our hearts make prayer;
Oh! aid us in our fond despair!
To Love--to Love alone our souls are given."

The two Tenors now went on, in duet; key of F minor:

"Oh! calm and holy night!
Those glowing worlds of light--
Heaven's eyes--begin to tread their mystic measure.
Soar high, like sweet bells far-off chime,
Night Hymn of Love, in silv'ry rhyme--
Beat at Heaven's gate, in rhythmic, pulsant measure."

At the words "soar high," etc., the music had gone into the key of D flat major, and now Lothair and Ottmar came in, in B flat minor:

"Oh! saintly souls above,
That burn in holy love,
With heart and tongue all pure from earthly tainting,

Drop down some balm on this poor heart,
Which fails, and droops, in bitter smart,
Contending here--in conflict well-nigh fainting."
Then, finally, the four voices ended in F major:
"Knock, knock, and soon the angel's voice will say,
'The gates are open! enter in for aye!'"

All of them--Lothair, Ottmar, and Cyprian--felt much affected by Theodore's lovely music, which was in the simple, serious style of the early masters. The tears came to their eyes. They embraced the clever composer; they pressed him to their hearts. The clocks tolled midnight.

"Blessed be our reunion!" cried Lothair. "Oh! glorious Serapion Brotherhood, which binds us with an eternal chain! May it ever keep green and flourish! As we have done to-night, we will continue to refresh and vivify our minds in the paths of literature and art; and our next care will be to assemble again here at our Theodore's, at the same time in the evening, this day week."